CONTENTS

NODDY

ANNUAL 2002

Pedigree

Published by Pedigree Books Limited
The Old Rectory, Matford Lane, Exeter, EX2 4PS.

E-mail books@pedigreegroup.co.uk

Published 2001

£6.99

WELCOME TO TOYLAND

HELLO, EVERYONE!

My name is Noddy and this is my little House-For-One. I live in a special place called Toy Town, in Toyland, and I have all sorts of adventures here with my red and yellow car. Would you like to hear all about them in this year's annual? All right, you shall, but first you must come and meet some of my nice friends - and some naughty goblins, who are not so nice...

NODDY'S CAR

Here is the little red and yellow car I told you about. It is the Toy Town taxi and we are usually very busy taking passengers for sixpence a ride. Everyone in Toyland knows the loud 'Parp! Parp!' of its horn!

BIG-EARS

This is my best friend, Big-Ears the Brownie. He lives in a toadstool house in Toadstool Wood and gets around Toy Town on his shiny red bicycle.

TESSIE BEAR

Tessie Bear is always kind to everyone, especially me. Her pet, Bumpy Dog is even more friendly. He is usually so pleased to see me that he knocks me right over!

MR. PLOD

The Toy Town policeman is usually busy trying to catch those naughty goblins. Mr. Plod may seem stern, but a good chocolate cake is sure to make him smile!

DINAH DOLL

Many of my passengers ask to go to Toy Town market, which is where Dinah Doll has a stall. If I ever have a spare moment between passengers, I always stop and see her.

MARTHA MONKEY

Martha, the toy monkey, often asks for a ride in my taxi. She's a little mischievous, though, and her love of sweeties sometimes gets her into trouble, as you will find out later!

MR. AND MRS. NOAH

Mr. and Mrs. Noah live in the Toy Town ark and take care of all the animals in it. Sometimes, one of the ark animals escapes and I have to bring them home in my taxi!

SLY

Sly is one of the naughty goblins who live in the Dark Wood near Toy Town. Although he and his friend, Gobbo, are always causing mischief, Mr. Plod always catches them in the end.

GOBBO

The only thing worse than a naughty goblin is two naughty goblins! If you should see Sly, Gobbo Goblin is usually not far away. Wherever there is a goblin, there is trouble!

TAXI!

If Big-Ears has a train to catch
Or Martha needs a lift,
Or maybe Mr. Wobbly Man
Would like to buy a gift,
If Mr. Jumbo wants some buns
And cannot walk that far,
They know they can ask Noddy
And his red and yellow car!

NODDY'S HOUSE-FOR-ONE

Noddy lives in Toy Town in his special House-For-One. Use your pencil to join up the dots and finish the picture, then colour it in with your favourite colours.

ONE FROSTY EVENING

One frosty evening, Tessie Bear went over to Noddy's little House-For-One.

Noddy was out. "I'll leave him a nice hot water bottle in his bed," she said.

A little later, Noddy came back and sat down on his bed to take off his shoes.

He felt something soft and warm. "There's an animal in my bed!" he cried, running out.

Noddy went to get Mr. and Mrs. Tubby Bear. "Look, there!" Noddy pointed.

Mr. Tubby Bear pulled the covers off the bed. "Come out of there!" he shouted.

Out flew the water bottle, right on to Mr. Tubby Bear's toe. "Ouch!" he cried.

"A hot water bottle!" Noddy exclaimed, blushing. How the Tubby Bears laughed!

ODDS AND EVENS

Noddy got quite a fright when he sat on the hot water bottle in his bed, didn't he? He really doesn't mind the cold weather, though, especially if it snows! Help him count the winter weather things below, then practise writing your numbers by going over the lines in pencil.
The numbers on this page are examples of odd numbers.

1

1 1 1 1 1 1

3

3 3 3 3 3 3

5

5 5 5 5 5 5

2 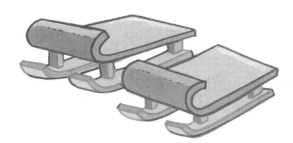 2 2 2 2 2

4  4 4 4 4 4

6  6 6 6 6 6

8   8 8 8 8 8

SNOWMAN

It doesn't really matter
If my teeth go 'chitter chatter',
I want to make a man out of snow,
I'll scoop and roll and pat,
And I'll find him a nice hat,
Then back to my warm house I will go.

A SNOWBALL RACE

Noddy, Master Tubby Bear and Martha Monkey are having snowball races down a hill. Can you see whose snowball has won this race? The answer is at the bottom of the page.

Answer: Martha's snowball has won the race.

NODDY'S CAR RUNS AWAY

Noddy is usually busy taking passengers around Toy Town in his little taxi, but sometimes he has time to stop for a tasty treat. What do you think he is going to eat?

Noddy loves ice-cream, and he knows that the ice-cream parlour on the hill sells the best in Toy Town. He parks his red and yellow car outside, making sure that the brakes are on properly and goes inside. He wonders which flavour he would like today.

Noddy asks for the biggest ice-cream in the shop and tries a spoonful. "Mmm, strawberry and banana - delicious!" he smiles. He is enjoying his treat so much that he does not notice two naughty little goblins peeping in at the door. What could they be up to?

"Let's get into Noddy's car while he's not looking!" sniggers Sly. "Yes," agrees Gobbo. "We can pretend to drive it while he's feeding his face!"

Sly and Gobbo clown around in the car. Suddenly, the car starts to move. "Put the brake back on!" cries Gobbo. "What's the brake?" Sly shouts back.

Noddy's car rolls faster and faster down the hill and the silly goblins have no idea how to stop it. They are very frightened that the car is going to crash. "Quick! Jump out!" yells Gobbo. He and Sly leap out of the car and land on the roadside with a BUMP!

The little car goes on and on down the hill at top speed. "Parp! Parp!" it hoots, to let people know it is coming. Look out, Mr. Plod! The policeman hears Noddy's car and sees it racing towards him. He jumps out of the way just in time. Away goes his helmet!

On goes Noddy's red and yellow car. The greengrocer is just on his way to market with some oranges. He hears a "Parp! Parp!" but his oranges are too heavy to move quickly. CRASH! The car knocks the oranges flying down the hill. The greengrocer is cross!

The poor little car still cannot stop. Mr. Milko cannot get to his cart in time. "Oh, my goodness!" he cries, as the car sends milk bottles everywhere.

Here come Mrs. Skittle and her family. "I can hear Noddy's car!" says one of the little Skittles. They don't know that Noddy is not in the driving seat!

Noddy's car bumped into the Skittles, sending them tumbling down the hill. "Oops-a-daisy!" chuckled Mrs. Skittle. "Down we go!" "Gosh!" exclaimed Mr. Jumbo, coming to see what was going on. "It's lucky that skittles are meant to fall over!"

Meanwhile, Noddy has finished his ice-cream and come out to get in his car. "My car! Where has it gone?" he cries. "I was just coming to tell you, Noddy," says Dinah Doll. "Those naughty goblins sent it running down the hill into town!"

Noddy rushed to Toy Town. "Oh, dear. What a mess!" he says, stepping over a milk bottle. "I must find my dear little car at once!"

Where do you think Noddy's car is? At the bottom of the hill is a pond and the car runs right into it. What a big splash it makes! A duck flies away in fright.

When Noddy gets to the bottom of the hill, there are lots of angry people waiting for him. "You're in a lot of trouble!" says Mr. Milko. "Where have you been, Noddy?" asks Mr. Plod, crossly. "I was just having an ice-cream," Noddy replies. "Where is my car?"

"Gurgle! Gurgle!" says Noddy's car, trying to hoot under the water. Noddy runs to the pond. "My poor car!" he gasps. "Someone get a rope!" Mr. Jumbo finds a rope and Noddy ties it to the car. They all pull with all their might until the car is safely out.

While Noddy dries his car, Dinah Doll speaks to Mr. Plod. "It wasn't Noddy's fault that his car did so much damage," she explains, "it was the goblins!"

When Mr. Plod hears how Sly and Gobbo got into Noddy's car and took the brakes off, he takes them off to the police station for a stern telling off.

Noddy helps the greengrocer and Mr. Milko to clear up the oranges and bottles. "And now I'd like all you Skittles to come back for tea," he says, "to make up for you having such a fright." The car takes everyone to Noddy's house - without bumping into a single thing!

ORANGES AND LEMONS

Noddy loves fruit and is buying some from the market. Luckily, the greengrocer has forgiven Noddy's car for knocking over his oranges! As well as oranges, the greengrocer is selling lots of other fruits.
Use your pencil to go over the letters below and practise writing their names. Which is your favourite fruit?

orange

banana

grapes

strawberry

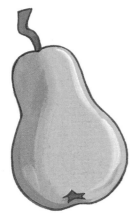

pear

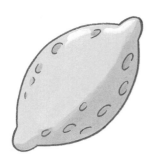

lemon

apple

IN THE GARAGE

People know Noddy's car
By the 'Parp! Parp!' of its horn,
It works hard, running passengers round town,
But once in a while,
Like any other car,
It's a nuisance to Noddy and breaks down!

He takes it to the garage,
But before very long,
Mr. Sparks says, "That's it, Noddy. Job's done!
It's a good little taxi
And now it's going fine,
Your red and yellow car will run and run!"

'C' FOR CAR

Here is Noddy's little car. The word car begins with the letter 'c'.
Look at the things below and use your crayons to
colour in any other words that begin with 'c'.

THE ROCKING CHAIR

Noddy was sitting in Big-Ears' old rocking chair. "I'm so tired!" he yawned.

Noddy rocked himself to and fro in the big chair. His eyes began to close.

Look what has happened! Big-Ears' rocking chair has turned into a boat!

The sea is very rough and the wind is strong. "Stop rocking!" cries Noddy.

It is so windy that the boat is blown up into the sky. Now it is an aeroplane!

Noddy does not like being blown about the stormy skies. "Stop rocking!" he cries.

Oh, poor little Noddy has been rocked out of the aeroplane! Down, down he falls...

...and lands with a bump! "You were just having a dream, Noddy!" chuckles Big-Ears.

READY TO DREAM

Little Noddy fell asleep in the rocking chair, didn't he? He might be more comfortable having dreams in his bed! Look at the things below and say which things Noddy might need at bedtime. Can you see anything that Noddy won't need at bedtime? Say when you think he would need it.

FUNNY DREAMS

A field full of flowers,
A fight with a bear,
A warm, sandy beach,
A wolf on the stair,
A house made of sweeties,
A fall from the swings,
A soft cloud to sit on,
A monster with wings...
Some dreams are scary,
Some are alright,
Sometimes I have none,
But some last all night!

NODDY WINS A PRIZE

One summer day, Noddy invited Big-Ears to his House-For-One for afternoon tea. "Hello, Big-Ears!" he called, as his friend cycled up. "I've made us a lovely chocolate cake! Come in and see!"

Noddy and Big-Ears sat at the table. "That is a nice cake, Noddy," smiled Big-Ears.
"Now, when we've finished, we must go into the garden and practise for the Toy
Town Sports Day." Noddy was surprised. "Sports?" he said. "I can't do sports!"

Over tea, Big-Ears explained that the only way anyone became good at sports
was through practice. Then he took Noddy into the garden and fixed up a rope
over the grass. "Let's start with jumping sports," he said. "See if you can jump
over that rope, Noddy."

Noddy was not sure he could jump that high, but he tried very hard. Oh, dear! His foot caught in the rope and down he went with a bump!

Big-Ears told Noddy he was no good at jumping and should try running instead. "You can't do that, either!" he exclaimed, timing Noddy's running.

Big-Ears said they would try the three-legged race next, and tied his right leg to Noddy's left one. "But I've got two legs!" Noddy pointed out. "If we run together, we have three between us," Big-Ears explained. The pair tried to run, but tumbled to the ground straight away!

Noddy decided he'd had enough of trying to do sports and went to bring the cake outside. "There is still one race you could go in for at the sports day," Big-Ears said thoughtfully, as he watched Noddy slice the cake. "It's called the egg and spoon race."

"I could easily beat a spoon in a race!" smiled Noddy. "Or an egg!" "That's not what I mean," said Big-Ears. He went to Noddy's kitchen and came back with an egg in a spoon. "You have to run along with it quickly, like this," he explained, showing Noddy what to do.

"I think I could do that, Big-Ears," said Noddy. He took the egg in the spoon and set off with it. "Slowly at first," Big-Ears told him. Noddy managed to go all round the garden before he dropped his egg. "Oh, it's broken!" he exclaimed. "That was my last one!"

Big-Ears told Noddy to wait while he went to get something. He came back with a wooden egg. "You can practise with this," he said. Noddy was pleased.

Noddy practised hard every day for the egg and spoon race. He could go faster and faster without dropping his egg. Can you see someone watching him?

It was Martha Monkey! She knew that the prize for the egg and spoon winner was a big jar of sweets and she had been practising hard, too. "It's not fair!" she said, crossly. "Noddy can do the race as well as I can. What if he wins? I shan't get my sweets!"

The day of the Toy Town Sports Day arrived and what do you think Martha Monkey did? She found a tube of glue and slipped it into her pocket. She was going to glue her egg to the spoon! "Now I'm sure to be able to go faster than Noddy," she chuckled.

It was time for the egg and spoon race. As everyone got ready to start, Noddy noticed Martha's glue. "What does she want with that?" he wondered.

Off went the egg and spoon runners. Of course, Martha Monkey came first and Noddy came second. "But how could Martha go so fast?" Noddy gasped.

Suddenly, Noddy realised why he had seen the glue behind Martha's back and was very cross indeed. He grabbed her spoon and turned it upside down. "Martha Monkey, you cheated!" he cried. Everyone gathered round. "Noddy, you won the race!" said Big-Ears.

Noddy was very pleased that he hadn't done all that practice for nothing.
Everyone cheered and clapped when he went up to get his prize from Mr. Sparks.
"There you go, Noddy," said Mr. Sparks. "Well done!" What an ENORMOUS jar of
sweets, Noddy!

Noddy knew that he would never be able to eat so many sweets all by himself,
so he opened them straight away and began to share them with his friends. If
Martha Monkey says she is sorry for cheating, perhaps Noddy will give her
some, too!

THE SACK RACE

Big-Ears managed to persuade Noddy to enter the sack race at the Toy Town Sports Day. Can you see who is winning the race? Who is second? Do you know who has fallen over with their sack? Who is holding the finishing tape? The prize for the winner of each race is a jar of yummy sweets. See if you can spot the five jars of sweets hidden in this picture. When you have found them all, use your crayons or felt-tip pens to colour in the picture.

BALL GAMES

Noddy didn't like running or jumping in the story, but he loves playing ball games. See if you can say which sport each of these balls is used for. The answers are at the bottom of the page.

Answers: a) tennis b) rugby c) basketball d) cricket e) football

SPORTS DAY

Can you run three-legged?
Can you race with a sack?
Can you dash for a bean bag
And carry it back?

Can you run really fast?
Can you hop on one leg?
Can you trot and keep balance
With a spoon and an egg?

Can you shout? Can you jump?
Can you just yell, 'Hooray!'?
Whatever you can do
You have fun on Sports Day!

MISS PINK CAT'S UMBRELLA

One day, Noddy stopped his taxi for Miss Pink Cat. She was hurrying to catch the train.

It began to rain. "Oh, my new hat!" Miss Pink Cat cried, putting up her umbrella.

It was so windy that Miss Pink Cat had to hold on to her big umbrella very tightly.

A gust of wind blew Miss Pink Cat right out of Noddy's taxi! "Parp! Parp!" cried the car.

Noddy followed Miss Pink Cat as she flew through the sky. "I'll catch you!" he called.

The wind began to drop and Miss Pink Cat almost fell into the river. Hurry, Noddy!

The wind gusted again and blew Miss Pink Cat towards the chugging Toyland train.

She landed right in it! After all that, Miss Pink Cat didn't catch the train - the train caught her!

A RAINY DAY

Big-Ears says, "Rain, go away!"
But I don't mind a rainy day,
The pitter patter of the rain
Upon my house's window pane
Just makes me open my door wide
And, in my wellies, run outside,
I see a puddle and off I dash
To jump in it and make a SPLASH!
I don't care that there's no sun,
I like the raindrops on my tongue,
I watch the ducks flap round in glee,
It's good for ducks, so it's good for me!

48

WELLY BOOTS

Noddy loves to splash about in the rain in his red wellington boots. Do you have a pair of wellies? What colour are they?
Choose your own design for the boots below and change them into a pair of wellies you would like to wear.

FIVE MORE MINUTES

My day's been so busy,
I'm ready for bed,
But I shan't go to sleep
Till my story's been read!

I know I keep yawning,
I'm tired, you see,
But first, could you please
Read a story to me...?

NODDY'S BEDTIME STORIES

Away Went Their Hats
The Clever Buttercup

AWAY WENT THEIR HATS

Big-Ears the Brownie was cycling home with lots of nice cakes for tea with his friends. Just as he rode round the big oak tree, a little gust of wind blew round him and whisked off his hat.

"Oh, bother!" said Big-Ears. He got off his bicycle and went to look for his hat, but it had disappeared. He was very cross, because he had to ride home without it.

That afternoon, Noddy was taking Mr. and Mrs. Noah to Big-Ears' house in his car. As he drove past the old oak tree, a sudden breeze blew his hat away, and Mr. and Mrs. Noah's hats, too!

"Stop, Noddy!" cried Mrs. Noah. "We've lost our hats!" Noddy stopped the car. "Mine's gone, too," he said. "I'll go and fetch them."

Noddy looked and looked, but he couldn't find any of the hats. "They're gone!" he called, and went back to the car, looking puzzled.

"How peculiar!" frowned Mr. Noah. "My head feels quite chilly now."

"Well, we mustn't be late," said Mrs. Noah. "Drive on, Noddy. We can always look for our hats later."

Big-Ears was most surprised to see his friends without their hats. "Goodness me!" he said. "My hat blew away in the wood, too!"

'Ting-a-ling-a-ling!' Along came Mr. Plod on his bicycle.

"I'm sorry I haven't got my helmet on," he said, leaning his bicycle against the fence. "But it came off as I was passing the old oak tree. Whoosh! Just like that!"

"That's what happened to us!" exclaimed Big-Ears, astonished.

"You should take the wind to the police station for a stern telling off, Mr. Plod," said Noddy, making everyone laugh.

"The strange thing is," frowned Mr. Plod, "I thought I heard a little giggle, just as my helmet came off. I've heard the wind whoosh and howl...but I can't say I've heard it giggle before."

"Well, Noddy can look for our hats on his way back," said Big-Ears.

"Yes," agreed Mr. Plod. He eyed the delicious cake. "It looks nice, Big-Ears. Chocolate cake with pink icing is my favourite!"

"I know. That's why I bought it," smiled Big-Ears. Mr. Plod beamed. He looked so unusually cheerful that Noddy wished he would have chocolate cake more often!

It was a lovely tea-party and everyone was sorry when it was time to say goodbye.

"Noddy, let the Noahs borrow your car," said Big-Ears, "and you go with Mr. Plod to look for our hats. I don't expect Mr. Plod wants to be seen in Toy Town without his helmet. He looks funny!"

When Noddy and Mr. Plod got to the oak tree, they looked under every bush and up in the trees for the hats. They could not find even one. Noddy was upset.

"I do miss hearing my bell go jingle-jing," he sighed. "What are we going to do, Mr. Plod?"

"I'll have to offer a reward," replied Mr. Plod, gloomily.

They went to the police station and Noddy watched as Mr. Plod wrote out a notice. He then put it up outside for him. It said:

LOST

Four hats and a helmet

A bag of sixpences offered for their return.

"Perhaps we'll get them back now," sighed Mr. Plod. "Goodbye, Noddy, and thank you for your help."

Would you believe it? The very next morning, Sly Goblin turned up at the police station with a sack. In it were all the hats...and Mr. Plod's helmet!

"That's better," Mr. Plod smiled, putting it on. "I feel like my old self again. So, where did you find them, Sly?"

"Oh...all over the place!" grinned the goblin. "The wind must have blown them away!"

"I knew that!" said Mr. Plod. "Here's your bag of sixpences."

"I wore your helmet for a little while," Sly giggled. "I did feel important!"

"What?" boomed Mr. Plod. "You dared to put on my helmet? You cheeky goblin!"

Sly ran off, giggling mischievously. A little later, Noddy came in.

"You found your helmet!" he cried. "Is my hat here, too?"

"Yes," replied Mr. Plod. "Here you are. Sly Goblin handed them in."

"But the bell's missing," Noddy said in alarm. "That naughty goblin must have kept it! I shall go and find him!"

Noddy hurried to his car and drove into the Dark Wood.

"Sly Goblin! Come out!" he called. "I want my bell back!" Noddy got out of his car and found the tree where Sly lived. He wasn't at home.

"He must be back in Toy Town," Noddy thought to himself, as he went in. Then he spotted his bell, shining brightly on a little shelf. Noddy went to grab it, then saw something else: a foot pump next to a book.

"What's this?" Noddy said to himself, picking up the book. "It's called 'Tricks With Pumps'." The book fell open at a well-thumbed page.

"How To Blow Hats Off Heads!" gasped Noddy. "It was Sly and his pump that blew our hats away, not the wind!"

Noddy picked up the things and raced to the door. He spotted the bag of sixpences on the table on his way out.

"I shall take that, too!" he said.

Noddy drove at top speed to the police station and ran inside.

"Mr. Plod!" he cried. "I found my bell in Sly's house, and look! He did a trick from this book to blow all our hats off! He must have been hiding in the old oak tree!"

"Then he brought the hats in to get the reward," frowned Mr. Plod, leafing through the book. "Wait till I get my hands on him!"

"Here's the reward," said Noddy, dropping the bag on Mr. Plod's desk.

"I got that back, too." Mr. Plod could hardly believe his eyes.

"Well done, Noddy!" he smiled. "I think you should have that reward - you've earned it!"

Noddy was delighted. He went and spent the sixpences on lots of cakes and drove through Toy Town, handing them out to all his friends.

"Parp! Parp!" tooted the little car.

"Sweets for everyone!" called Noddy. "Come and get your sweets!"

As for Sly Goblin, there wouldn't be any sweets where he was going: to the police station, for a stern telling off!

THE CLEVER BUTTERCUP

Noddy arrived at Big-Ears' toadstool house one morning and was surprised to see five little rabbits playing in the garden.

"What are you doing here?" he asked them. "You should be playing in the woods!"

Big-Ears opened his window and peered out.

"Which one of you rabbits has taken my butter?" he shouted, crossly. "It was on my larder shelf and now it's gone!"
Noddy shut the gate so that the rabbits could not run away.
"Who took Big-Ears' butter?" he asked, sternly.
"We don't like butter!" squealed all the rabbits.
"Well, I'm sure I've seen one of you having buttered scones in the tea-shop," frowned Noddy. "Which one of you was it?"
"Not me! Not me! Not me! Not me! Not me!" cried each of the rabbits in turn. Big-Ears came out.
"One of you has definitely had my butter," he said. "Line up in a row, please."
The rabbits lined up, nudging each other and giggling mischievously. Big-Ears went down the row to see if he could spot any buttery whiskers, but he could not.
"We told you we didn't like butter!" they all cried.
"One of you must like it," Noddy insisted. "You must own up. Who is it?"

"Not me! Not me! Not me! Not me! Not me!"

"I see," said Big-Ears. "Noddy, go and pick the biggest buttercup you can find. There are some in the little meadow at the end of that path over there."

Noddy ran down the path and came out in the meadow. He found a beautiful big buttercup, as golden as the sun, and looked into its gleaming cup.

"You're so nice and shiny," Noddy smiled, "you look as if you've been polished." He took the flower back to Big-Ears.

"Now," said Big-Ears, holding up the buttercup. "All of you hold your chins up."

Noddy watched as his friend took the buttercup and held it under each furry little chin in turn.

"My buttercup has told me who the butter thief is," he told them at last.

"Who is it?" the rabbits cried.

"It's Snuffles, here," Big-Ears

replied, pointing to one of the rabbits. "Isn't it, Snuffles? I shall be telling your mummy what you've been up to."

Snuffles burst into tears.

"Please don't tell my mummy!" he sobbed. "I can give you the butter back. Look!"

The naughty rabbit ran to a corner of the garden and lifted up a cabbage leaf. There was the butter, hidden away until Snuffles could sneak it out of Big-Ears' garden.

"It was by the window," he sniffed, bringing it back. "The window was open, so I took it. We don't have it at home because I'm the only one who likes it. I couldn't help taking it."

"You could help it," Big-Ears frowned. "You know you mustn't just take things. If you had asked me nicely, I would have given you some butter. Now you haven't had any at all. If you say sorry, I shan't tell your mummy."

"I'm very sorry, Big-Ears," said Snuffles. "It won't happen again."

"All right," Big-Ears gave a little smile.

"Did the buttercup really tell you it was me?" Snuffles asked.

"Of course," replied Big-Ears.

"How did it?" Noddy asked, as puzzled as Snuffles.

Big-Ears gave Noddy the golden buttercup.

"Hold it up to each rabbit's chin," he said. "If a patch of gold appears, that rabbit loves butter."

Noddy went down the line of rabbits, holding the yellow flower under each little chin. When he reached Snuffles, a patch of gold shone out on his furry chin. Snuffles was the only one who liked butter!

The rabbits hopped away, whispering to each other about the magic buttercup. Noddy held the flower up to Big-Ears' chin and a bright yellow patch glowed there at once.

"You really like butter, Big-Ears!" he chuckled. "See if I do!" Big-Ears took the buttercup and held it under Noddy's chin. A golden light shone there, too.

"You love butter as well, Noddy," smiled Big-Ears, "but we didn't need the buttercup to tell us that. Who ate four currant buns with butter at tea the other day?"

"I did!" said Noddy. "Oh, Big-Ears, did I really pick a magic buttercup?"

"All buttercups have this magic in them," Big-Ears explained. "Try another one and see."

Noddy fetched another pretty buttercup from the meadow and tried it. Big-Ears was right! Next time you see some buttercups, pick one and you shall see the golden magic for yourself!

BED!

My story's told, I've had my kiss
And now it's time for bed,
I think I'll plump my pillow up
Before I rest my head.
I've said goodnight,
I'm all curled up,
I've checked my nightlight's on,
I hope I have exciting dreams
That last the whole
night long!

NODDY'S MAGIC BUTTERCUP

When Noddy went to look for more buttercups, he found all sorts of pretty flowers. Can you say which of the flowers below is a magic buttercup? What are the names of the other flowers? The answers are at the bottom of the page.

a

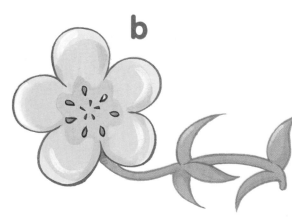

b

c

d

e

67

COUNT THE SPOTS

When Noddy was looking for magic buttercups, he found some ladybirds, too. Count the number of spots on each of his ladybirds, then write the number in the box.

ARK ANIMALS

Some are big,
Some are small,
Some are short,
Some are tall,
Some are spotty,
Some are plain,
Some are stripy,
Some have a mane.

Some hop, some bounce,
Some trot, some crawl,
But Mr. Noah loves them all!

WHERE'S MY MUMMY?

Mrs. Noah is very pleased because some of the ark animals have had babies. Can you match up each of the babies with their mummies? Which of the babies has lost his mummy?

Sometimes there is a special name for a baby animal. A baby lion is called a cub. Can you say what the other babies are called? The answers are at the bottom of the page.

Answers: The baby bear (also called a cub) has lost his mummy; a baby duck is a duckling, a baby sheep is a lamb and a baby horse is a foal.

KATIE KANGAROO TRIES TO HELP

One morning, Noddy bought lots of nice things to eat from Dinah Doll's stall.

When he got to his car, he realised he had no basket to put his shopping in.

Watch your shopping, Noddy! There goes an egg, and some sausages, too.

What should Noddy do? "You can use my pouch, Noddy!" says Katie Kangaroo.

What a useful tummy pocket Katie has. Everything fits in. "Thank you," says Noddy.

When they reach the ark, Katie gets out and says goodbye. "But -" Noddy begins.

It is too late. Katie forgets about the shopping and bounces off, right over the ark!

Noddy's shopping is ruined. Now he must go and buy it all again! Poor little Noddy!

BOUNCY SHADOWS

Katie Kangaroo never stops bouncing! Look at the shadows below and say which shadow exactly matches the colour picture of Katie. The answer is at the bottom of the page.

1

2

3

4

74

KATIE KANGAROO

Of all the animals in the ark,
One is sure to make Bumpy Dog bark,
For she can bounce even higher than he,
She could, if she wanted, jump over a tree!
She's brown, with a pouch - can you guess who?
That's right, it's Katie, the ark's kangaroo!

NODDY'S BAG OF MONEY

Noddy was having a very busy Friday in his taxi. First he took Miss Pink Cat to her uncle's, then he dropped Mr. Tubby Bear at the station. Can you see who his next passenger was?

Noddy's next passenger was Mr. Wobbly Man. "Take me to the market, please, Noddy," he said. "I've a lot of things to buy." When Noddy had dropped him there, he took Mrs. Skittle to fetch her children from nursery school. He did have a lot of passengers!

At lunchtime, Noddy went back to his little House-For-One to count up all his sixpences. Goodness me, what a lot of money he had earned that week! He put all the coins in a bag and tied it up so that he could go and buy some things in Toy Town.

Noddy went out to his car and put the bag of money on the back seat. "I need some petrol," he said to himself. "I think I shall go to Mr. Sparks' garage first."

On his way to the garage, Noddy saw Gobbo Goblin. "Oh, he's waving at me," said Noddy. "I suppose I shall have to stop and pick him up."

Noddy stopped the car and Gobbo jumped in. "I'm in a hurry, Gobbo," said Noddy. "Where do you want to go?" "To the station, please," Gobbo smiled. As the car set off, he spotted the bag of money and smiled even more. "Actually, Noddy, I'll just get out here," he said.

"But you've only just got in," Noddy said, as he stopped the car. "Changed my mind," Gobbo said, leaping out again. "That's still sixpence," Noddy sniffed.

Gobbo gave Noddy sixpence. "Goodbye, then," frowned Noddy, driving away. Gobbo sneaked off with the money under his coat. What a naughty goblin!

Noddy drove straight to the Toy Town garage and asked Mr. Sparks to fill the car with petrol. "Of course, Noddy," smiled Mr. Sparks. Noddy went to get some money from his bag so he could pay for it. "Oh, no!" he cried. "My money! It's gone!"

Mr. Sparks could see that Noddy was very upset. "Don't worry, Noddy," he said. "You can pay me another time." Poor Noddy said goodbye and drove off.

Noddy hoped that he would get lots of passengers to make up for the money he had lost, but no one wanted a taxi all afternoon. He was fed up!

Noddy couldn't even buy anything for tea. He went to see Big-Ears and told him about his missing money. "Come and eat with me," Big-Ears smiled, "and tell me what happened." Noddy sat down and told his friend who his passengers had been that day.

When Noddy had finished, Big-Ears nodded knowingly. "Don't you see, Noddy?" he said. "That naughty goblin must have taken your money!"

Everyone was very kind to little Noddy when they heard that his money had been stolen. Mrs. Tubby Bear invited him round for breakfast the next morning.

When he left the Tubby Bears' house, Noddy saw Mr. Milko. "Here, Noddy," he said, giving him two bottles of milk. "No charge today." "Thanks!" Noddy smiled.

Noddy dropped in to see Tessie Bear. "I heard what happened," Tessie smiled, "so I've made some buns." Even Bumpy Dog tried to give Noddy one of his bones!

Noddy thanked Tessie Bear and went home. A few moments later, there was a knock at the door. There stood Mr. Plod with naughty Gobbo. "Mr. Sparks tells me your money was stolen, Noddy," the policeman said sternly. "That's right," Noddy agreed.

"This goblin would like to give you it back and apologise," said Mr. Plod, prodding the goblin in the ribs. "Sorry," mumbled Gobbo, holding out the money bag.

"My money!" cried Noddy, delighted. "You got it back! Thank you so much, Mr Plod." Mr. Plod took Gobbo away to the police station for a stern telling off.

Noddy ran to Tessie Bear's house to tell her the good news. "Look, Tessie!" he cried. "Mr. Plod got my money back from Gobbo Goblin! Everyone has been so kind, I think I shall have a party for you all!" Bumpy Dog barked and bounded around in excitement.

Noddy had a tea party at Tessie Bears house and invited everyone who had helped him when he had no money. "This is a lovely tea, Noddy," said Tessie Bear. "Yes, thank you," added Big-Ears. "Thank you," replied Noddy, "for being such good friends!"

MONEY, MONEY, MONEY!

Look at all the coins Gobbo stole from Noddy! He has counted them and there are 20 altogether. He has tried to number them, but has missed some numbers out. See if you can fill them in with your pencil or pen.

WHO DID THAT?

If ever there's trouble in Toy Town
Everyone knows who's to blame,
If ever there's something gone missing,
They know who is playing a game,
If it's broken or spoilt or knocked over,
Or someone has started to cry,
The whole town knows just who to look for:
Those goblins, Gobbo and Sly!

NAUGHTY GOBBO GOBLIN

Join in the story by saying what the pictures are as they appear.

Naughty stole a from . He decided

to take the into Toy Town and buy himself lots of

nice things. Suddenly, bumped into and

the dropped out of his jacket. looked at

the sixpences on the ground. "That's Noddy's missing

 ," he said sternly. He made go and see

 to give back the . Little was very

pleased and said he would look after his more

carefully in future.

A FLAT TYRE

Oh, dear! Somebody has left drawing pins in the road and poor Noddy now has a flat tyre. Who do you think could have played such a naughty trick? Could it be one of those mischievous goblins?

Look at the two pictures and see if you can spot the 5 differences between them. The answers are at the bottom of the page. Then use your crayons or felt-tips to colour in the pictures.

87

Answer: In bottom picture – Beetle has rucksack There are less drawing pins on the floor. There are only two trees on the hill. Gobbo is holding a bag not a box. There are no mushrooms at the base of the tree.

THE NAUGHTY GOBLINS

Noddy and Tessie Bear were building sandcastles on the beach.

Sly and Gobbo saw them and came to spoil their fun. What naughty goblins!

When they had finished jumping on the sandcastles, they scared away the seagulls.

Tessie Bear started to cry. Noddy shouted at the naughty goblins and chased them away.

Later that afternoon, the goblins fell asleep. They were tired from causing all that mischief!

The seagulls spotted Sly and Gobbo. One flew down and picked up Gobbo's hat in its beak.

Down flew three more seagulls and took Sly's hat and belt and Gobbo's handkerchief.

"It serves you right!" Noddy called to the cross goblins. "Now leave us to play in peace!"

LOST PROPERTY

Every Friday, Mr. Plod sorts out the things that have been handed in to Toy Town police station. The special name for these things is 'lost property'. It looks like a few people have lost some property this week! Help Mr. Plod by saying who you think has dropped each of the things below. The answers are at the bottom of the page.

a

b

c

d

90

HERE TO HELP

He may be large,
He may look stern,
But help is what he'll give,
If you're in trouble
Or you've got lost,
Just tell him where you live,
He'll start to smile,
He'll take you home,
He's very kind indeed,
If you're out playing
And things go wrong,
A policeman's all you need!

HELLO, DINAH DOLL

This is Dinah Doll. Whenever Noddy goes to Toy Town market, he always visits Dinah's stall and finds something that he likes.

Use your crayons or felt-tip pens to colour in this picture of Dinah Doll.
See if you can match the colours to those on the opposite page.

NODDY AND THE HONEY

One autumn afternoon, Mr. Noah asked Noddy to go into the Toyland countryside and pick up 20 jars of honey from the Honey Lady. He wanted the honey as a treat for the bears in his ark.

The Honey Lady came out of her cottage when she heard the 'Parp! Parp!' of Noddy's car. "Hello, Noddy!" she called. "I'll bring out Mr. Noah's order for you!" The Honey Lady helped Noddy to put all the jars in his car. "The bears will love this," said Noddy.

Noddy said thank you to the Honey Lady and set off back to the ark. He had to drive through the woods, where the wind was blowing the leaves off the trees. "Goodness me, it's rather windy today," little Noddy said to himself as he went along.

Suddenly, a ball bounced out of the trees on to the road. Noddy tried to steer round it, but Sly Goblin ran out on the road, too. Poor Noddy did not know which way to go! He swerved this way and that, trying to get his car under control. Look out, Noddy!

CRASH! Noddy's car ran right into a tree and rolled on to its side. BUMP! Noddy fell out of the car into the honey that had spilt everywhere. Sly Goblin picked up his ball. He knew the crash was his fault, so he ran away and hid. Can you see him?

Noddy was not hurt, but covered in honey. Goodness me, what a sticky mess he was in! He could not even ring his bell, it was so gummed up!

Zzzzzz! Zzzzzz! What was that noise? Noddy looked up and saw lots of bees. They could smell the honey and wanted some. "Oh, no!" cried Noddy.

Noddy didn't like so many bees buzzing round him. The noise they made was very loud and he began to feel afraid. "Go away!" he shouted, as he began to run away. "Go away and find your own honey!" Noddy ran quickly, but the bees still chased him.

Noddy raced through the wood. As he looked back to see if the bees were still following him, he caught his foot in a tree root. Over he went with a bump!

Noddy rolled through a big pile of leaves that had fallen from the trees. The bees hung overhead and buzzed crossly, wondering where their honey had gone.

Noddy got up and tried to brush the leaves away, but they were all stuck to the honey on his clothes. Many of the bees flew off, but some still buzzed around Noddy's head. He ran on until he saw Big-Ears' house. He would go there for help.

Big-Ears came out and stared in alarm at the strange person there. "Who are you? Go away!" he cried, and chased Noddy away before he could reply.

On his way home, Noddy saw Master Tubby Bear in his garden. "A scarecrow!" cried Master Tubby Bear. "Shoo! Away from our garden!"

Noddy decided he should just go home. As he got there, he saw Bert Monkey and said hello. "A leaf monster!" cried Bert Monkey, running away. "Help!"

Noddy went inside. When he caught sight of himself in the mirror, even he got a fright. "What's happened?" he wailed. "I've turned into something horrid!"

Just then, there was a knock at the door and Tessie Bear came in. "Tessie!" said Noddy. Tessie Bear knew by his voice that the funny leaf person was Noddy.

Tessie Bear was not a bit frightened. As she pulled the leaves off one by one, he told her what had happened. She counted more than a hundred leaves!

Tessie Bear told Noddy to have a bath and wash away the sticky honey. Meanwhile, she found him some clean clothes. "That's better!" she smiled, when he had finished. "You look more like yourself. Now you must get dressed so we can fetch your car."

"Look!" Noddy said delightedly, when he found his car. "Someone's turned it the right way up!" "And it's nice and clean!" added Tessie.

The car was pleased to see Noddy. "Parp! Parp!" it hooted. "I'm glad you're all right," smiled Noddy. "Now we must fetch some more honey for the bears!"

"Noddy!" Big-Ears hurried over. "I found your car on its side, covered in honey, so I cleaned it up. What happened?" Tessie told him that the funny leaf person he'd chased away earlier was Noddy, covered in honey and leaves. Big-Ears did feel silly!

BACK TO THE HIVE

Now that those bees have finished chasing Noddy, they need to find their way back to the Honey Lady. Show them the way back through the woods so that they can settle in their hives again and make more honey for the bears!

HOME, SWEET HOME

Look at the Toyland people on this page, then look at the homes on the facing page and see if you can match them up. The answers are at the bottom of the page.

What sort of a home do you live in? Where would you live if you could live anywhere at all in the world?

Big-Ears and Whiskers

Noddy

The Honey Lady

Mr. and Mrs. Noah

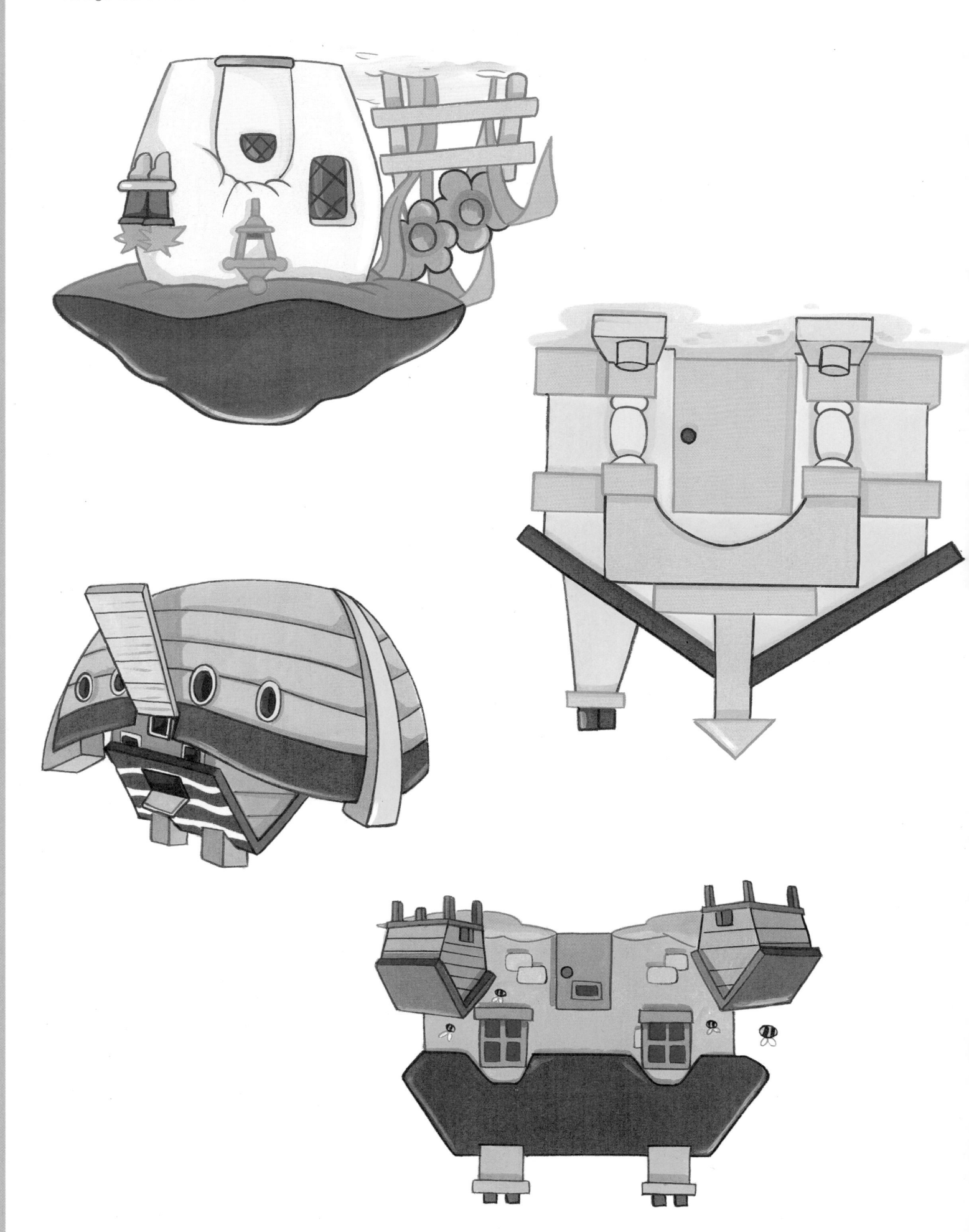

NODDY AND THE HELTER-SKELTER

Big-Ears told Noddy that the fair was in town. Noddy wanted to drive there straight away.

Noddy loves the fair and was excited when he arrived. He wanted to go on everything first!

"Look!" Noddy cried. "A helter-skelter! I've always wanted to go on one of those!"

The helter-skelter was very high. Noddy was not really sure that he wanted to go down it.

Noddy was stuck at the top of the slide. Big-Ears knew a way of persuading him to come down!

Noddy said he was too afraid to slide down. "Don't you want this ice-cream, then?" asked Big-Ears.

Noddy loves ice-cream even more than he loves fairs. He took a deep breath, then let go.

Noddy sped down and knocked Big-Ears over. Now he must wait a little longer for his treat!

HONEY FOR TEA

Gobbo tries to steal your honey. Speed on two spaces to escape

Start

1

2

19 18 17 16

A friendly rabbit shows you a short-cut. Go on two spaces.

20

You have a puncture. Miss a go while Mr. Sparks mends it.

21

22 23 24

Someone's dropped an ice-cream in the road. Skid on two spaces!

Now Noddy has finally got his honey, he and Big-Ears can take it to the bears in time for tea! You and a friend can join him on his journey to the ark if you can find a dice and two counters.

Decide who is going to be Noddy and who is going to be Big-Ears, then put your counters on the start. Take turns to throw the dice and work your way round Toyland, making sure you throw a six to start. The first one to reach the ark with their honey is the winner!

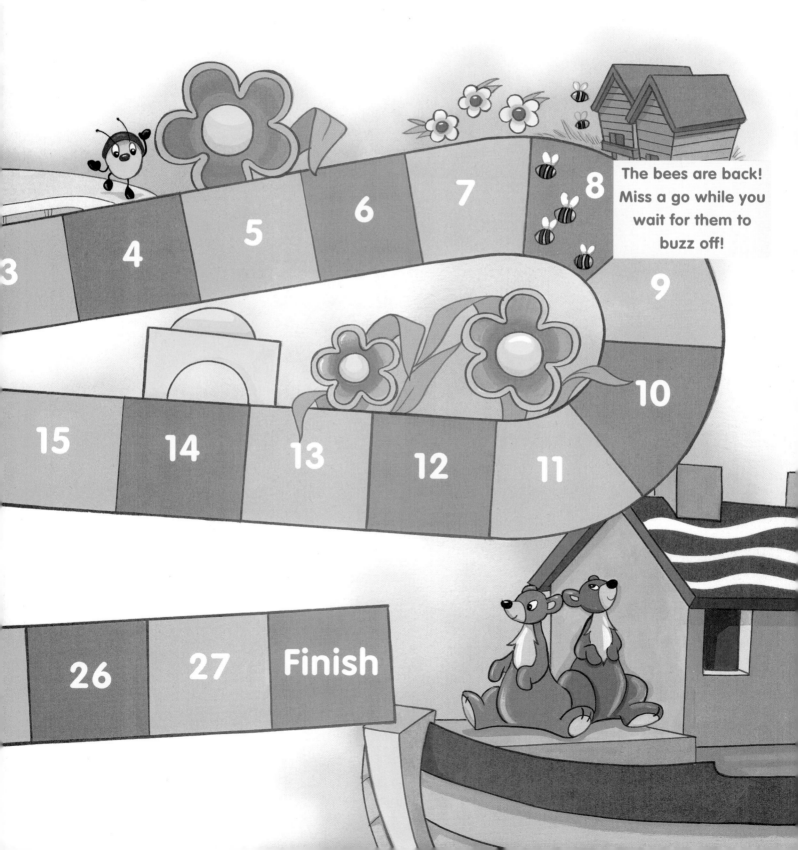

The bees are back! Miss a go while you wait for them to buzz off!